The Fox and the Crow

Manasi Subramaniam
Culpeo S. Fox

When dusk falls, they
arrive, raucous, clamping
their feet on the wires in
a many-pronged attack.

As Crow makes to join
them, a wafting scent
gives him pause.

BAKERY

Thief!

BAKERY

Bread is best eaten
by twilight.

But a pair of eyes
glitters dangerously
from the dark edges
of the woods.

Fox sneaks towards Crow
- she always sneaks.

Their eyes meet, a challenge is spoken.

When the moon slithers
into the open skies,
surely some trickery
is afoot.

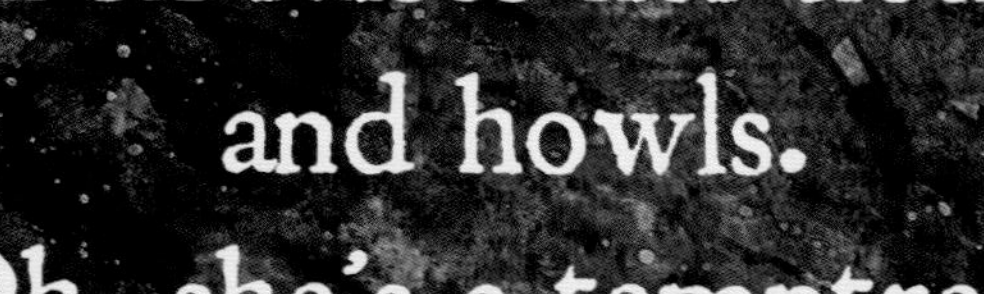

Fox raises her neck
and howls.
Oh, she's a temptress,
that one.

A song is
an invitation.
Crow must
sing back.

From mouth
to mouth
- a song
and a piece
of bread.

Crow's pride sets
his hunger ablaze.
Fox smirks.

Fox's tail teases as she swishes away.
Crow's stomach burns with
swallowed song.

A new day breaks. An old hunger aches.

The Fox and the Crow

Author: Manasi Subramaniam
Illustrator: Culpeo S. Fox

Karadi Tales Company Pvt. Ltd.
3A Dev Regency 11 First Main Road Gandhinagar Adyar Chennai 600020
Ph: +91 44 4205 4243 Email: contact@karaditales.com
Website: www.karaditales.com

Distributed in North America by Consortium Book Sales & Distribution
The Keg House 34 Thirteenth Avenue NE Suite 101 Minneapolis MN 55413-1006 USA
Orders: (+1) 731-423-1550; orderentry@perseusbooks.com
Electronic ordering via PUBNET (SAN 631760X); Website: www.cbsd.com

Printed in India
ISBN No.: 978-81-8190-303-7